The Wrong Fairy Tale

GOLDiLOCKS
and the Three Little Pigs

First American Edition 2021
Kane Miller, A Division of EDC Publishing

A Raspberry Book
Art direction and cover design: Sidonie Beresford-Browne
Internal design: Sidonie Beresford-Browne & Ailsa Cullen
Copyright © Raspberry Books Ltd 2020

For information contact:
Kane Miller, A Division of EDC Publishing
P.O. Box 470663,
Tulsa, OK 74147-0663
www.kanemiller.com
www.usbornebooksandmore.com

Library of Congress Control Number: 2020936359

Printed in China
ISBN: 978-1-68464-160-4
2 3 4 5 6 7 8 9 10

The Wrong Fairy Tale

By Tracey Turner
and Summer Macon

GOLDiLOCKS
and the Three Little Pigs

Kane Miller
A DIVISION OF EDC PUBLISHING

Once upon a time, in the Land of Fairy Tales, a girl called Goldilocks was out for a walk in the woods when she spotted a little house made of bricks. She'd never noticed it before, and, being a curious sort of girl, she went to have a closer look.

There was a sign nailed to the garden gate:

NOTICE
TO WOLVES
GO AWAY

"Well, I'm not a wolf," said Goldilocks to herself as she opened the gate and walked up the garden path. "It can't do any harm to say hello."

She knocked loudly on the front door
three times and waited.
There was no answer.

"Hello!" called Goldilocks. She thought she
heard a squealy-snorty sort of noise, but then
it went quiet. "Anybody home?" she called,
giving the front door a little push. To her
surprise, it swung open. A delicious smell
came wafting through the door.
Goldilocks' tummy rumbled.

Meanwhile, in their little brick house, the Three Little Pigs had heard footsteps on the garden path and shut themselves inside a cupboard in a panic.

"It's the Big Bad Wolf!" said the First Little Pig. "He'll be asking to be let in in a minute!"

"And then he'll start huffing and puffing!" said the Second Little Pig.

"I'm sure there's nothing to worry about," said the Third Little Pig. "Not in this fine brick house. But let's stay in here, just in case."

But instead of the Big Bad Wolf's booming voice . . .

Knock!
Knock!
Knock!

"What's going on?" said the First Little Pig.

"What about, 'Little pigs, little pigs,
let me in'?" said the
Second Little Pig.

"Well, whatever happens, he won't get
into this house," said the Third Little Pig.
"It's made of bricks!"

Then, with a creak, the front door of the brick house swung open.
Goldilocks stepped inside.

"Is anybody there?" she said, looking straight at the
cupboard. She marched up to it and opened the door . . .

and three
frightened
little pigs
tumbled out.

"You're not the **Big Bad Wolf!**" snorted the Second Little Pig, squeezing out from underneath the Third Little Pig. The First Little Pig ran to the front door and drew two hefty bolts across it.

"No, of course I'm not," said Goldilocks. "I just wanted to say hello to my new neighbors, and . . . oooh, is that porridge?"

There were three delicious-smelling bowls on the table.
"Would you mind?" Goldilocks asked. Without waiting for an
answer, she picked up a spoon and dipped it into the first bowl.

"But—" began the First Little Pig.
"Oh! That's far too hot," exclaimed
Goldilocks, and picked up the
spoon next to the second bowl.

"No, that one's too cold," she said,
moving on to the third bowl.
"Wait!" said the Second Little Pig.

"Mmm! This one is just right!" said Goldilocks happily,
taking another spoonful from the third bowl.

"Hang on," said the First Little Pig. "A blond girl goes into
a cottage in the woods, she finds three bowls of delicious pig swill . . ."

"You're Goldilocks!" said the Three Little Pigs together.
"You're in the wrong fairy tale!"

Goldilocks spun around. "Oh!" she said, with a worried
look at her spoon. "What happens now?"
As if in reply, a great booming, bark-y sort of
voice shouted from outside:

Little pigs!
Little pigs!!
Let me in!

"It's the **Big Bad Wolf!**" squealed the Third Little Pig.

"NO!"

shouted all Three Little Pigs. "You cannot come in.
Not by the hair on our chinny-chin-chins!"

"Luckily, I built MY house out of bricks," the Third Little Pig told Goldilocks. "And not from puny sticks or—and I can scarcely believe anyone would do this—straw."

"Luckily, someone remembered to lock the front door this time," muttered the First Little Pig, who was busy closing all the window shutters.

Outside, the Big Bad Wolf was huffing, and puffing, and doing his best to blow down the brick house.

"Ha!" laughed the Third Little Pig nervously. "He'll never blow down this house!"

After a lot more huffing and puffing, the Big Bad Wolf rattled the front door and the window shutters, growling angrily.
"I'll show you and your brick house, piggies!" snarled the wolf. "I'll get in there somehow."

The First Little Pig had his eye to a hole in one of the shutters.

"He's got the ladder!" he said.

"The chimney!" squealed the Second Little Pig.

"Come on!" cried Goldilocks. She ran to the fireplace.

"Here," said the First Little Pig, handing
Goldilocks a bundle of straw. "This was left over
from when I built my straw house." Goldilocks
used the dry straw to start the fire.

Thump! Bash!

There was a thunk as the ladder
slammed against the side of the house.
"He's climbing up to the roof!" oinked the Second Little Pig.
"Quick, take these. They were left over from my stick house."
Goldilocks added the sticks to the little fire one by one.
They crackled and burned.

BANG!

The **Big Bad Wolf** was on the roof. "Come on, Goldilocks!" squeaked the Third Little Pig, handing her a log from the log basket.

Smash!

A roof tile fell and splintered to pieces outside.

"There!" said Goldilocks. "That should do it!"
Orange flames burned brightly in the fireplace.
A moment passed before a big, furry, bushy tail appeared
at the top of the hearth. The flames licked higher . . .

"...wwwww!"

howled the Big Bad Wolf, scrambling back up the chimney with his tail on fire. He popped out of the chimney, leapt off the roof, barely touching the ladder, put out his tail in the garden pond, and bounded off into the distance.

"Well, I don't think we'll be seeing him again," said Goldilocks. And she was right—the Big Bad Wolf never came anywhere near the little brick house ever again. Goldilocks and the Three Little Pigs became great friends, and they all lived happily ever after.

Even though it was completely
the **WRONG FAIRY TALE.**

THE END